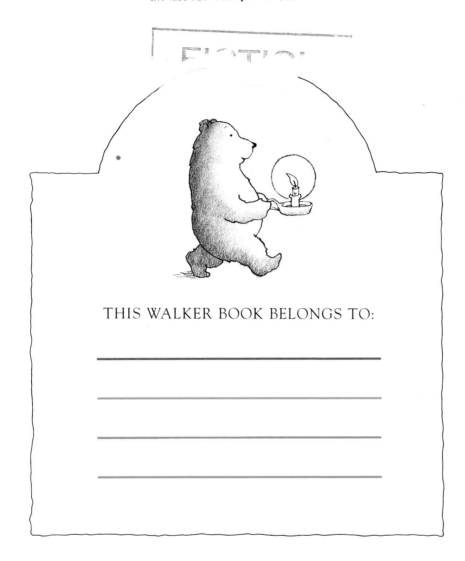

THIS WALKER BOOK BELONGS TO:

_____

_____

_____

_____

For Nana and Grandad

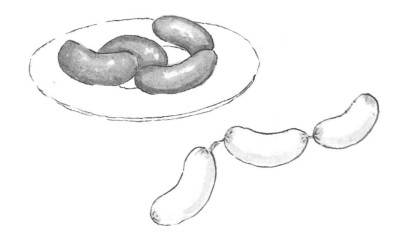

First published 1993 by Walker Books Ltd
87 Vauxhall Walk, London SE11 5HJ

This edition published 1995

4 6 8 10 9 7 5

© 1993 Siobhan Dodds

This book has been typeset in Garamond.

Printed in Hong Kong

British Library Cataloguing in Publication Data
A catalogue record for this book is
available from the British Library.

ISBN 0-7445-3631-6

Grandad Pot
Siobhan Dodds

WALKER BOOKS
AND SUBSIDIARIES
LONDON • BOSTON • SYDNEY

ring
ring
ring

"Hello, Grandad Pot.
Mummy said I could
come to tea and stay
the night and if I'm
good you might make
me a chocolate cake.
Chocolate cake is
my favourite food.
Don't worry, Grandad Pot –
I won't be any trouble."

What a surprise for Grandad Pot!
Polly is coming to stay.

Quick, quick, quick!
A chocolate cake for Polly.

ring
ring
ring

"Hello, Grandad Pot.
Can Henry come too?
He won't be any trouble.
Henry has a big plaster
on his knee. He was
doing cartwheels in the garden and he
fell over. He didn't cry. He told me that
jelly and ice-cream will make his knee
better. Don't worry, Grandad Pot.
Henry can sleep in my bed."

What a surprise for
Grandad Pot!
Henry is coming
to stay.

Quick, quick, quick!
Jelly and ice-cream for Henry.
Oh! and a chocolate cake
for Polly.

ring
ring
ring

"Hello, Grandad Pot.
Can Rosie come too?
She won't be any trouble.
Rosie isn't feeling very
well today. I think she
has a cold. She sneezed four
times this morning. She likes
banana sandwiches best. Don't worry,
Grandad Pot. Rosie can
sleep in my bed too."

What a surprise for
Grandad Pot! Rosie
is coming
to stay.

Quick, quick, quick!
Banana sandwiches for Rosie.
Jelly and ice-cream for Henry.
Oh! and a chocolate cake
for Polly.

ring
ring
ring

"Hello, Grandad Pot.
Can George come too?
He won't be any trouble.
George has red spotted
shorts and a big, fat tummy.
His favourite food is sausages.
Don't worry, Grandad Pot.
George can sleep in
my bed too."

What a surprise
for Grandad Pot!
George is
coming
to stay.

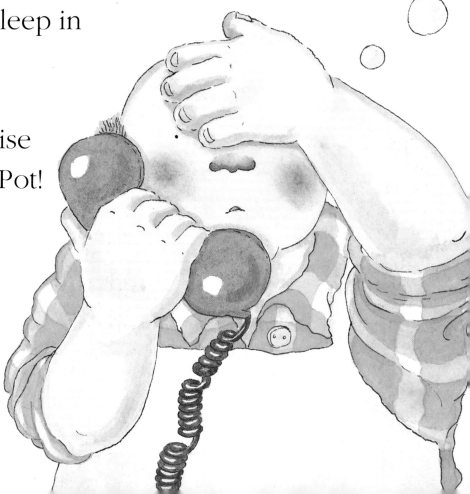

Quick, quick, quick!
Sausages for George.
Banana sandwiches for Rosie.
Jelly and ice-cream for Henry.
Oh! and a chocolate cake
for Polly.

Knock
Knock
Knock

"Hello, Grandad Pot.
This is Henry,
this is Rosie,
and this is George."

What a surprise
for Grandad Pot!
Oh! and …

what an enormous tea for Polly!

"Goodnight, Grandad Pot.
It's lots of fun coming to stay."

MORE WALKER PAPERBACKS
For You to Enjoy

ROSIE'S FISHING TRIP
by Amy Hest/Paul Howard

One morning very early Rosie and her grandad set off on a fishing trip together.
They have a fine time, but they don't come back with any fish!

"The harmony between the old and the very young has not often
been shown as effectively as it is here." *The Junior Bookshelf*

0-7445-4703-2   £4.99

THE WILD WOODS
by Simon James

When Jess takes a walk in the woods with Grandad, she discovers some
natural wonders and learns a lesson too about wild things.

"A breath of fresh air… Witty and sparkling line-and-wash pictures…
Full of humour and vitality." *The Guardian*

0-7445-3661-8   £4.99

THE TRAIN RIDE
by June Crebbin/Stephen Lambert

What could be finer than a train ride with Mum across country to the sea,
where someone very special is waiting – Grandma!

"There's lots to see, both on the bright red steam train and through its windows, with bold,
strongly coloured illustrations of a hazy summer's day sweeping across
the pages to draw you into the rhyme." *Practical Parenting*

0-7445-4701-6   £4.99